D1412276

Raccoon's *Adventure*

in Alphabet Town

by Janet McDonnell
illustrated by Helen Endres

created by Wing Park Publishers

CHILDRENS PRESS®
CHICAGO

Library of Congress Cataloging-in-Publication Data

McDonnell, Janet, 1962-
Raccoon's adventure in Alphabet Town / by Janet McDonnell ; illustrated by Helen Endres.
p. cm. — (Read around Alphabet Town)
Summary: Raccoon meets "r" words on his adventure in Alphabet Town. Includes activities.
ISBN 0-516-05418-X
[1. Alphabet—Fiction. 2. Raccoons—Fiction.] I. Endres, Helen, ill. II. Title. III. Series.
PZ7.M478436Rac 1992
[E]—dc 20
92-1066
CIP
AC

Printed in the United States of America.
1 2 3 4 5 6 7 8 9 10 11 12 R 98 97 96 95 94 93 92

Raccoon's ***Adventure***

in Alphabet Town

You are now entering Alphabet Town,
With houses from "A" to "Z."
I'm going on an "R" adventure today,
So come along with me.

This is the "R" house of Alphabet Town. Raccoon lives here.

Raccoon likes "r" things. His house is filled with them.

Raccoon likes to ride a

roller coaster.

And he likes to run races.

Most of the time, he is a good little raccoon. But sometimes, Raccoon is a rascal.

One day, Raccoon was walking
down the

road

that leads to the market.

He saw

Rabbit

coming. She had a big basket of red berries. Raccoon loved red berries.

He began to think like a rascal.
"I will trick Rabbit," said Raccoon.
"Then I will get her red berries."

Raccoon ran home. He found a rope and a rattle.

He drew a face on the rope.

Then he ran back to the road. He threw the rope on the road and hid behind a

rock.

When Rabbit walked by, Raccoon shook the rattle. "Eeek!" said Rabbit. "A rattlesnake!"

Rabbit dropped her basket and ran away.

"I think Raccoon needs to learn a lesson," said Robin. Off she went to tell Rabbit her plan.

Then she went to visit a real rattlesnake. She told him her plan too. "I will help you," said Rattlesnake.

Rattlesnake crawled to the rock where Raccoon was hiding. Then he shook the rattle on his tail.

"Eeek!" said Raccoon. "A real rattlesnake!"

He ran as fast as he could, all the way home.

When he got to his house, Rabbit was waiting. "You tricked me," Rabbit said.

"You are right," said Raccoon. "I have been a real rascal. I am sorry. Please forgive me."

Raccoon showed Rabbit where he hid her red berries. "I promise not to be a rascal anymore," he said.

"All right," said Rabbit. "Then you may share my red berries with me."

And that is how Raccoon and Rabbit became real friends.

MORE FUN WITH RACCOON

What's in a Name?

In my "r" adventure, you read many "r" words. My name begins with an "R." Many of my friends' names begin with "R" too. Here are a few.

Do you know other names that begin with "R"?
Does your name begin with "R"?

Raccoon's Word Hunt

I like to hunt for words with "r" in them. Can you help me find the words on this page that begin with "r"? How many are there? Can you read the words?

Can you find any words with "r" in the middle?
Can you find any with "r" at the end?
Can you find a word with no "r"?

Raccoon's Favorite Things

''R'' is my favorite letter. I love ''r'' things. Can you guess why? You can find some of my favorite ''r'' things in my house on page 7. How many ''r'' things can you find there? Can you think of more ''r'' things?

Now you make up an ''R'' adventure!